Catacomb Rescue

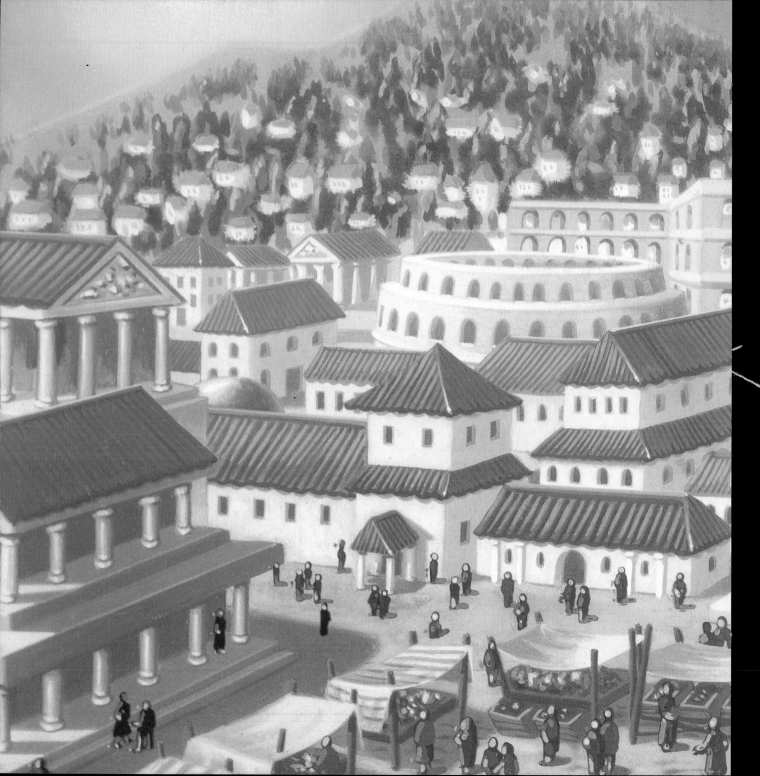

THE STORY
KEEPERS

Episode
3

Catacomb Rescue

Brian Brown and Andrew Melrose

CASSELL

Cassell
Wellington House, 125 Strand,
London WC2R 0BB

© Brian Brown and
Andrew Melrose, 1996

First published 1996

**British Library Cataloguing-
in-Publication Data**
A catalogue record for this
book is available from the
British Library.

ISBN 0-304-34687-X

Long ago, in the city of Rome,
there lived a mighty ruler.
His name was Nero.
He thought he was a god,
but the Christians knew he wasn't.
So Nero hated them.

One day there was a great fire.
Nero said the Christians started it,
and he sent his cruel soldiers after them.

Marcus, Justin, and Anna
lost their parents during the fire.
Ben the baker and his wife, Helena,
took them into their home.
There, in a time of great danger,
they told the children stories about Jesus.

This book is about the adventures
of the Storykeepers.

Ben, Helena, and the children were sneaking
through the streets of Rome.

"Careful, everyone," Ben warned.
"We don't want to be seen.
Tonight you will meet Ephraim,
who was once with Jesus.
The soldiers would love to capture him."
Finally the group reached the secret meeting place.

"Ephraim!" Ben greeted his old friend.
"We are eager to hear your story!"
Ephraim laughed. "All right," he said.
And he began to tell this story.

One day a lawyer asked
Jesus, "How should I live?"
Jesus told this story.
A Jew was traveling down a
road. Some men robbed him and
beat him up. They left him to die.

A temple priest saw the man.
But he did not stop to help.
Another man from the temple did not stop either.
But a Samaritan felt sorry for him.
He stopped and put the man on his own donkey.

The Samaritan took him to an inn and looked after him. The innkeeper was surprised.
"Usually Samaritans and Jews do not speak to each other," he said, "but this Samaritan helped a Jew."

Jesus asked the lawyer: "Which of these people showed us how to live?"
The lawyer answered, "The one who was kind to him."
"Do the same," said Jesus.

Anna and Justin listened carefully
to the story.
One of Nero's spies heard the story.
He told Nero about Ephraim.
Nero was furious.
"Find this man!" he ordered. "Search
every house in Rome. Close the gates.
No one may leave the city."

The next day Justin burst into the bakery.
"The soldiers are coming!" he cried.
"We've got to hide Ephraim!"
"Justin and Anna," said Ben, "take Ephraim
to the catacombs. Wait for me there.
And take these papers. They will help Ephraim
get out of the city."

After the soldiers had gone,
Ben made his way to the catacombs.
It was dark. He thought no one saw him.

But two soldiers,
Tacticus and Nihilus,
were following him.
They watched him
go in.

Ben found Ephraim and the children.
They hurried through the tunnels
of the catacombs.

Suddenly Ben heard a noise.
He turned and saw two shadows.
"We're being followed! Run!" he called.

"You go on with the children, Ben,"
said Ephraim. "It's me they're after."
"I'll carry you, old friend," said Ben.
But the soldiers were catching up.
"I have an idea," said Anna.
She kicked the wall of
the catacomb.

Rocks began to fall. Then the roof fell in.
But a wall of rocks separated Ben and Ephraim
from the children.
"I know another way out," said Anna.
"Go ahead without us."

Justin and Anna heard a voice behind them in the tunnel.

"Nihilus! Help me!" Tacticus called.

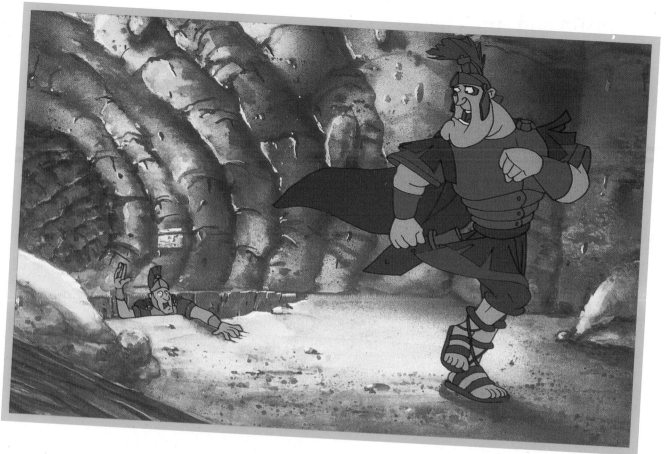

He had fallen into a pit.
But Nihilus ran away.
"Help yourself!" he shouted back.

"It's one of the soldiers.
He's trapped," said Justin.

Anna was frightened.

"What should we do?" she asked.

"Leave him," said Justin.

"Nihilus, help me please!" called the soldier.

"It's not right to leave him," said Anna.

"But he was going to arrest us," said Justin.

Anna felt sorry for
the soldier.
She grabbed his whip
to pull him out.
But she could not
hold on. She slipped.
Justin grabbed and
pulled.

Together the children pulled him out.
But they dropped Ephraim's papers.

Tacticus groaned.
"Are you all right?" asked Anna.
Tacticus rubbed the dirt
from his eyes.
He stared at
the children.

"You? You saved me?" he cried.
"But you are Christians.
I came in here to arrest you.
Why would you help me?"

"We were just doing what the Samaritan
did," said Anna.
"What Samaritan?" Tacticus asked.
"In the story Ephraim told," Anna said.
"Take me to Ephraim," said Tacticus.

Outside the catacombs,
a crowd of people had gathered.
"We must go and fight the soldiers,"
someone said.
Ephraim was calming them down.
"We must learn to forgive," he said.
He told them another story Jesus told.

There was a servant who owed his king
a lot of money.
He could not pay it back.
"You must sell all you have," said the king.
"Give me time, I'll pay," said the man.
The king felt sorry for the servant.
He forgave him and let him go.

Then the servant met a friend who owed him money.
"Pay me what you owe!" he cried.
"I need more time!" the friend begged.
But the servant had him thrown into prison.

When the king heard about this he was angry.
"I let you off," he said, "but you did not do the same for your friend."
And he threw the man into prison.

"We must forgive those who hurt us," Ephraim concluded.
Just then Tacticus stepped forward.
"Are you Ephraim, the Christian storykeeper?" he asked.
"Did you tell these children the story of the Samaritan?
Another soldier left me to die, but because of your story
these children saved my life."

Tacticus
became
friends with
all the Christians
from that day.
"I will help you all I
can," he told Ben.
"I will make sure that Ephraim gets out
of Rome safely."

And Tacticus kept his word.

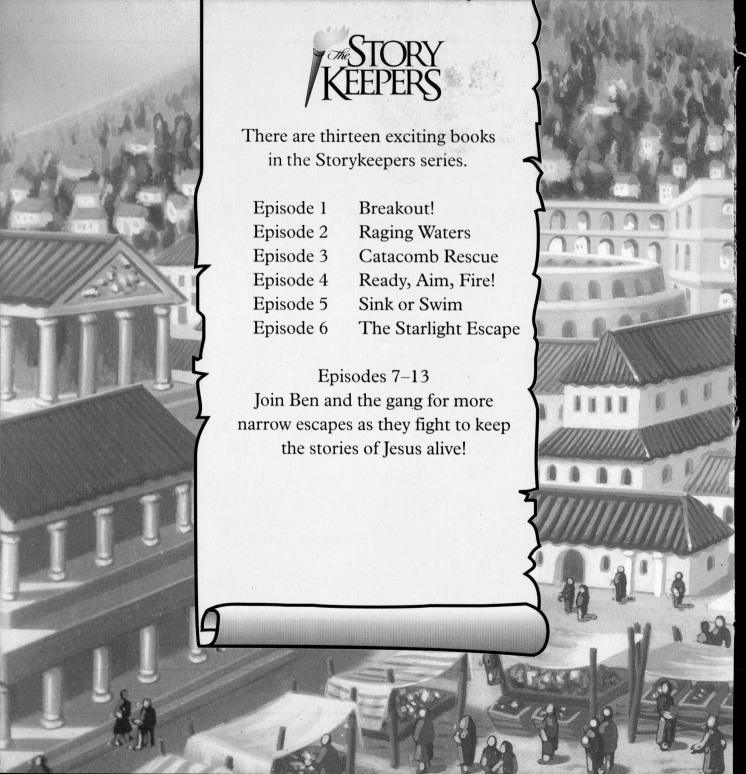

THE STORY KEEPERS

There are thirteen exciting books
in the Storykeepers series.

Episode 1   Breakout!
Episode 2   Raging Waters
Episode 3   Catacomb Rescue
Episode 4   Ready, Aim, Fire!
Episode 5   Sink or Swim
Episode 6   The Starlight Escape

Episodes 7–13
Join Ben and the gang for more
narrow escapes as they fight to keep
the stories of Jesus alive!